Printed in the U.S.A.

ISBN 0-7172-8267-8

JIM HENSON'S MUPPETS

IN

Kermit and the
New Bicycle

A Book About Honesty

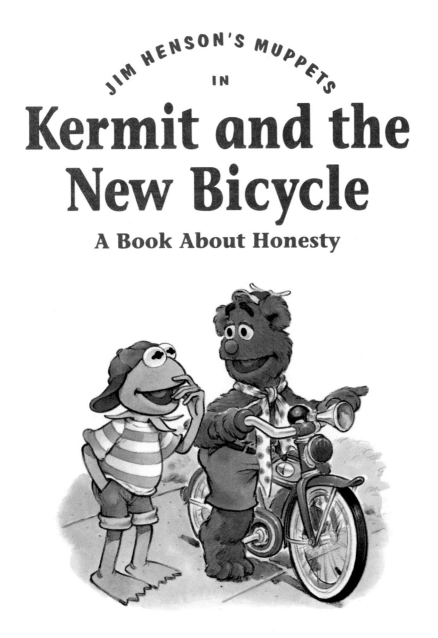

By Michaela Muntean • Illustrated by Joe Ewers

GROLIER

"Wow," said Kermit.

"Great, isn't it?" said Fozzie.

"It sure is," Kermit agreed as he circled Fozzie's new bicycle. The fenders were a bright, shiny blue, and the chrome on the spokes and handlebars winked and sparkled in the sunlight.

Fozzie squeezed the horn attached to the handlebars. It made a kind of wheezing, honking sound. "It's the best birthday present ever," he said happily.

"Ever," echoed Kermit.

"Want to take it for a spin?" Fozzie asked.

"You bet I do," said Kermit, and he hopped on the bicycle and pedaled down the block.

He was back in a few minutes. "It rides like a dream," said Kermit. "You sure are lucky."

"You can ride it anytime you like," said Fozzie as he got on the bike. "Bye, Kermit!"

"Happy birthday, Fozzie," Kermit called.

As Fozzie rode away, Kermit thought about how great it would be to have a brand-new bicycle. Of course, Fozzie *had* said Kermit could ride his anytime. Kermit decided that if he couldn't have a new bike himself, the next best thing was having a good friend with a new bike —especially one who lived next door.

The next day, Kermit saw Fozzie wheeling his new bike out of the garage. "I'm off to Scooter and Skeeter's house," he called. "See you later, Kermit!"

"Okay," Kermit answered. "I've got some chores to finish. Stop by on your way back!"

Fozzie nodded, waved, and pedaled away.

Later, when Kermit had finished his chores, Fozzie was nowhere to be found. Then Kermit noticed that the Bear family's car was gone and that the brand-new bicycle was back in the garage. *Fozzie must have gone somewhere with his parents,* thought Kermit.

He looked at the bicycle. "It sure is a beauty," he said to himself.

Kermit lifted one leg over the bar and straddled the seat. He sat like that for a few minutes. "Fozzie *did* say I could ride it anytime I wanted to, so . . . what am I waiting for?" Kermit asked himself. And because he couldn't think of a good answer, he wheeled the bike around and glided down the driveway.

Kermit started slowly. He pedaled gently. He steered carefully.

One block, two blocks—and then Kermit grew daring. He pedaled harder, and the harder he pedaled, the faster he went. He whizzed past trees and houses. He was going full speed when he turned the corner, and that must have been why he lost control of the bike.

The next thing Kermit knew, he was on the ground, and the bicycle—Fozzie's brand-new blue bicycle—was lying on the ground, too, its front wheel horribly bent out of shape.

"Oh, no," Kermit groaned. He had a terrible, sick feeling in the pit of his stomach. His knee was scratched, but that didn't matter—it hurt more to look at the scratches on the shiny blue fender of Fozzie's new bike.

Kermit brushed himself off and started the long walk home, carefully wheeling the bike alongside. As he walked, he tried to think of a way to tell Fozzie what had happened. He wasn't sure how he was going to do it, but there was one thing he *was* sure of—it wasn't going to be easy.

The closer he got to Fozzie's house, the sicker he felt. He just couldn't face Fozzie. Then Kermit thought of something he *could* do, and so he turned the bike around and headed toward town.

It was a long six blocks to Bud's Bike Shop, but Kermit would have walked sixty if there were any way the bike could be fixed right away.

Bud looked at the bike. "I'll have to order a new wheel and repaint the fender," he said. "You could have it back in a week."

Kermit asked how much it would cost, and when Bud told him, Kermit gulped. He'd need to do a lot of chores to make that much money.

"If I bring you everything I have in my piggy bank, can you start work on it right away?" Kermit asked.

"Well..." Bud hesitated.

"Please," said Kermit. "I'll work hard to pay you the rest of the money."

"Okay," Bud agreed. "You can come back in a week to pick it up."

"Thanks," said Kermit.

Kermit felt better knowing the bike would be fixed, but the hardest part was yet to come—telling Fozzie. As Kermit got closer to home, that sick feeling returned to the pit of his stomach. He'd just have to tell the truth, no matter how hard it was going to be. But then, as he was walking the last block, he saw Fozzie.

"Kermit," Fozzie cried. "Someone's taken my bike!"

Kermit just stared at Fozzie. "But…er…ah," Kermit began. He tried to speak, but the right words wouldn't come. Finally, instead of telling the truth, Kermit said, "That's terrible."

"Who would do such a thing?" Fozzie wailed.

"I don't know," said Kermit, because now that the lie was out, he didn't know how to get it back.

For the rest of the afternoon, Kermit helped Fozzie look for his bike.

"I'll probably never see it again," Fozzie said sadly.

"Maybe you will," Kermit said. "Maybe the person who took it will bring it back."

"Do you really think so?" Fozzie asked hopefully.

Kermit didn't know what to say, so he just nodded. It was easier not to talk. He could feel the lie growing larger with every word.

Kermit tossed and turned all night. The next morning, he woke up early and set to work. He raked his neighbor's lawn. He swept the sidewalk. He ran errands for his mother. Then he went to look for more work.

"Gee, Kermit," Fozzie said when he saw him that afternoon. "You sure are busy today."

"I need to earn some extra money," Kermit said.

"I'd better get some jobs, too," said Fozzie, "so I can afford to buy a new bike. I don't *really* think anyone will bring mine back."

Suddenly Kermit couldn't stand it any longer. "Fozzie, I've got something to tell you," he blurted out.

Kermit told Fozzie the whole story. He told him he'd taken the bike and how it had crashed. He told him the bike was being repaired. Then he told him how sorry he was.

When Kermit finished, Fozzie was quiet. "Why didn't you tell me before?" he finally asked.

"I *wanted* to," said Kermit. "But I was afraid you'd be mad at me. Then, after I lied to you the first time, it got harder and harder to tell the truth. Pretty soon, I didn't know *what* to do. Can you ever forgive me?"

"I've already forgiven you," said Fozzie. "You're my best friend, and I know you meant to do the right thing. But lies can cause big problems, even between friends. So let's promise that we'll always tell each other the truth—no matter what."

"You bet," Kermit agreed. *"No matter what."*

Let's Talk About Honesty

Kermit certainly got into a lot of trouble by not telling the truth, didn't he? But he learned a big lesson, too. It's a whole lot easier to tell the truth from the beginning!

Here are some questions about honesty for you to think about:

Have you ever told a lie?

If you have, how did you feel afterward?

Were you afraid to tell the truth? Why?